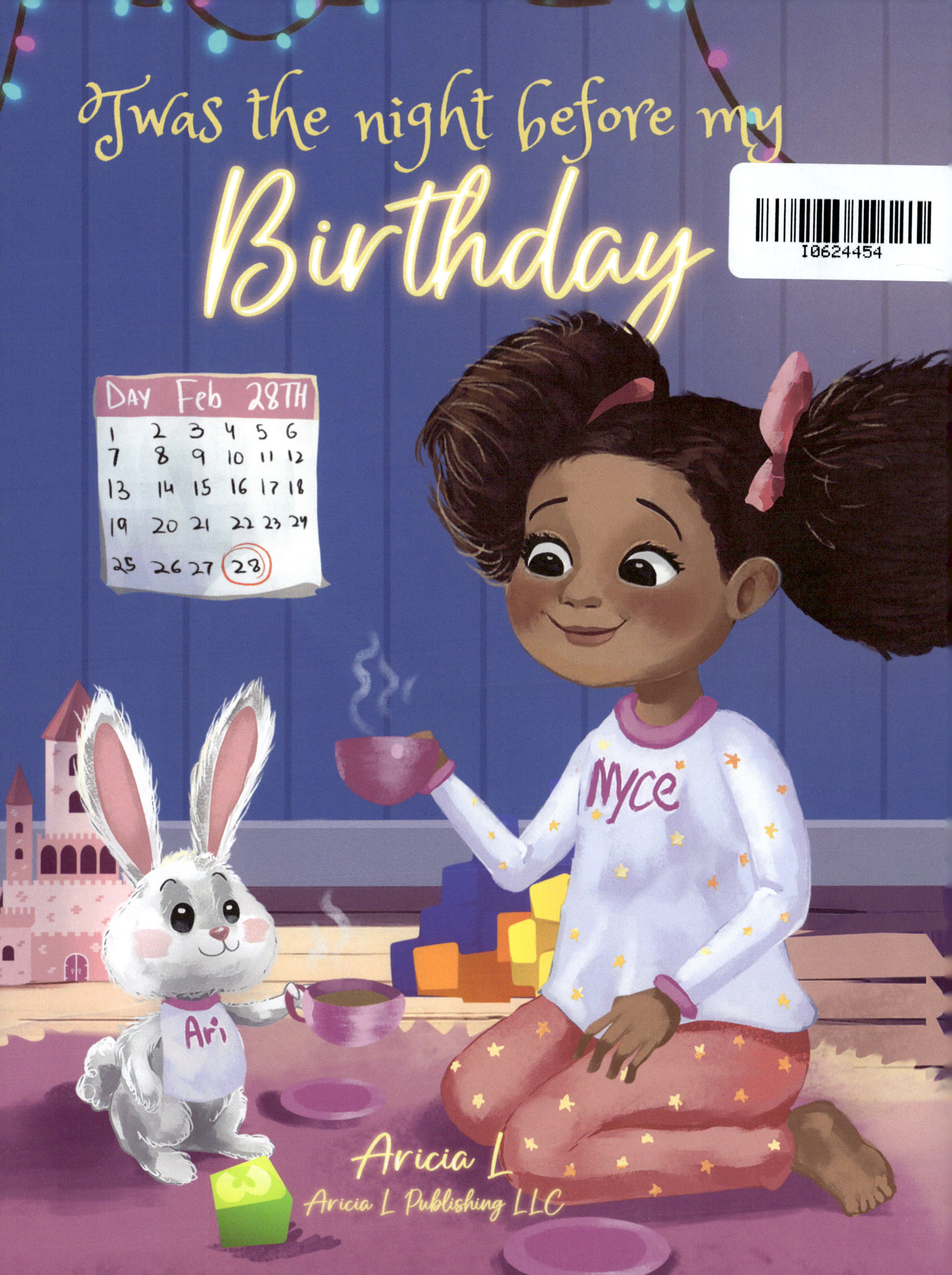

DEDICATION

THIS BOOK IS DEDICATED TO AERIN, ARIAH, AND JAYDEN, WHOSE BRIGHT SPIRITS INSPIRE ME EVERY DAY. TO THE REST OF MY FAMILY, THANK YOU FOR YOUR UNWAVERING LOVE AND SUPPORT. TO ALL THE INCREDIBLE KIDS I'VE HAD THE PRIVILEGE OF WORKING WITH OR COACHING, YOU CONTINUE TO TEACH ME VALUABLE LESSONS. AND MOST IMPORTANTLY, TO YOU, THE READER: MAY THIS BOOK SPARK YOUR IMAGINATION AND REMIND YOU THAT ANYTHING IS POSSIBLE WITH DEDICATION AND A TOUCH OF MAGIC. ALWAYS REMEMBER TO LEAVE A LITTLE SPARKLE WHEREVER YOU GO!

'Twas the night before my birthday, before I hopped into bed.

I sat at my table
with my bunny Nyce instead,
To talk and gossip about my big day ahead.

So I poured his tea and passed him his cake. I shared how it will feel to be 8.

To imagine waking up, on my very special day, With Nyce in my arms all ready to play.

Excited to hear people say, "Happy Birthday Ari" "How old are you?"

For then me to say, with a little sass and a grin,

Putting up 8 fingers, with a twirl and a spin, "I'm 8!"

Jumping out of bed and to my surprise,

Hopefully, see a giant box with something special inside

To open the box and out pops glitter, rainbows and butterflies,

To then reach down and pull out my surprise,

A big giant unicorn that has gleam in her eyes.

She has a sparkly dress that is fit for a queen.

She is so cute and oh so clean.

We spin and we twirl, then fall to the ground.

I think how special this day has already went down.

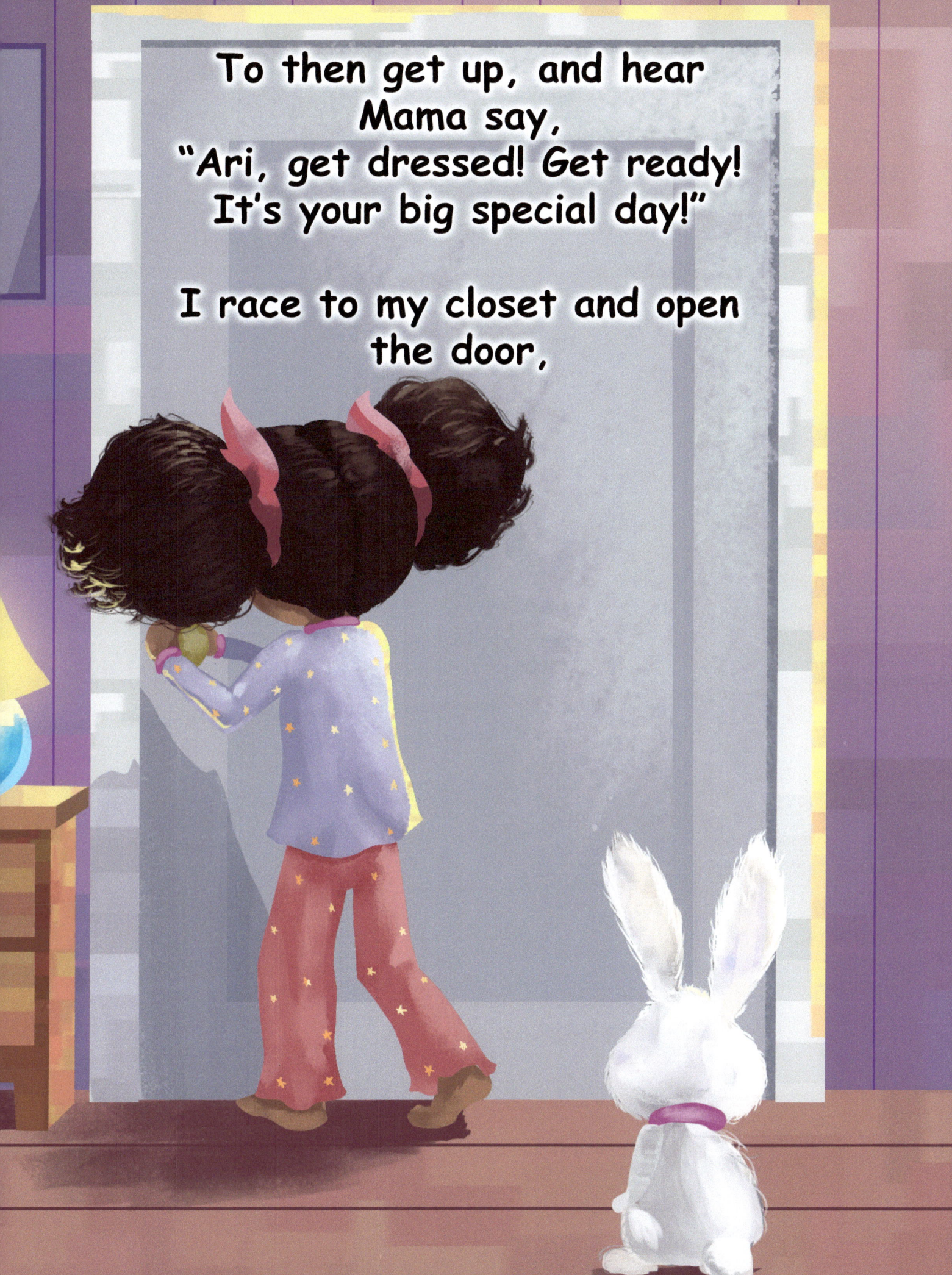

To then get up, and hear
Mama say,
"Ari, get dressed! Get ready!
It's your big special day!"

I race to my closet and open
the door,

To find the most amazing colored rainbow dress,

That is so long it touched the floor. Beside it is a little colorful tux, So small and so cute.

Racing to my bed to grab my bunny,
screaming "I'm 8! I'm 8! I'm 8!"

All dressed to the nines,
we are ready to go.

I open my door and to my surprise,

A long glitter carpet, that is very long inside.

So I skip down the carpet, happily.
As I skip down the carpet, the lights grow deem.
It is really quiet and oh so grim.

To see the lights pop on and to my surprise,
All my friends and family gather close inside.
Singing "Happy Birthday Ari"
"How old are you?"

Seeing Mom holding a
big pink frosted cake,
The cake is so tall
I almost didn't see the 8.

With 8 long candles sparkling so bright, With a sparkle in my eye and a twirl and a spin, I blow them all out, like a gust in the wind.

Oh wow, I can't wait!
So now Nyce and I,
Will hop into bed.

While I count some sheep
that dance in my head.
I tuck us in and kiss Nyce
good night.

I think to myself,
For tonight, I go to sleep 7,
When I wake,

I'll be 8!!!

The End

ABOUT THE AUTHOR

BORN INTO A MILITARY FAMILY AND MARRIED TO A SERVICE MEMBER, ARICIA L HAS JOURNEYED ACROSS THE GLOBE, WITH HER LATEST DESTINATION BEING NEW JERSEY. SHE IS A DEVOTED MOTHER OF TWO SONS AND A DAUGHTER, AND A LOVING AUNT TO A NEPHEW.

ARICIA'S DEDICATION TO CHILDREN EXTENDS FAR BEYOND HER FAMILY. WHILE STATIONED OVERSEAS, SHE VOLUNTEERED EXTENSIVELY AT DEPARTMENT OF DEFENSE SCHOOLS AND COACHED VARIOUS SPORTS, ENRICHING THE LIVES OF MILITARY CHILDREN.

HER PASSION FOR WORKING WITH CHILDREN EVOLVED INTO A FULFILLING CAREER. TODAY, ARICIA WORKS WITH CHILDREN ON THE AUTISM SPECTRUM WHO FACE BEHAVIORAL CHALLENGES, INCLUDING THOSE WHO ARE NONVERBAL. HER UNWAVERING DEDICATION AND EMPATHY INSPIRE BOTH HER STUDENTS AND COLLEAGUES. THIS SAME PASSION HAS IGNITED ARICIA'S IMAGINATION, LEADING HER TO EXPLORE THE WORLD OF WRITING.